Wallykazam!™

Dragon Hiccups

Adapted by Kristen L. Depken • Illustrated by Benjamin Burch
Based on the episode "Dragon Hiccups" by Adam Peltzman

A GOLDEN BOOK • NEW YORK

randomhousekids.com

ISBN 978-0-553-52310-2

Printed in the United States of America   10 9 8 7 6 5 4 3 2 1

One day while Wally and Norville were playing, Norville made a strange sound, and fire came out of his nose! He had the dragon hiccups!

"Don't worry, buddy," said Wally. "We can fix this."

Norville stood on his head.

He held his breath.

But his hiccups wouldn't go away!

Wally thought a drink of water might make the hiccups disappear. He waved his magic stick and shouted, "Water!" But nothing happened. The magic words that day had to rhyme with **bash**.

"**Splash!**" said Wally, and a splash of water landed in Norville's mouth.

Norville kept hiccupping, so Wally took him to see Ogre Doug.
"There's a cure!" said Ogre Doug.

He handed Wally a list and a beaker. "You just have
to find these five things. Then put them in this beaker,
mix them up, and put a little drop on Norville's nose."

First on the list was a thread from an ogre's pants. Doug was an ogre, and he was wearing pants! He plucked off a thread and dropped it into Wally's beaker.

Next, they needed a potato from a giant.

"I know where to get that!" said Wally. He and Norville headed to Gina Giant's house.

On the way, Bobgoblin heard them. He decided that he would scare Norville to make his hiccups go away.

"Dandelions are scary," said Bobgoblin. He picked a handful and ran after Wally and Norville.

Wally and Norville arrived at Gina Giant's house.

"We need a giant potato," said Wally. "Do you have one?"

"Of course I do!" said Gina. She gladly gave them a giant potato.

crash

The potato was so big, it started to roll down the hill! Wally needed a magic word that rhymed with **bash** to make it stop.

"Crash!" shouted Wally as he waved his stick. A wall popped up just in time for the potato to crash into it.

mash

But the potato started bouncing right toward Wally and Norville!

"Wallykazam! Wallykazato!" cried Wally. "Give me a word to stop this potato!" His magic stick made the word **mash** appear.

"Mash!" shouted Wally. With that, the giant potato turned into mashed potatoes!

Splat! The mashed potatoes landed on Wally and Norville. Wally put some in his beaker.
Next on the list: a pinch of mud from a swamp.

Suddenly, Bobgoblin popped out
from behind a rock. He waved a bunch
of dandelions in front of Norville to
scare the hiccups away.

"Dandelions aren't scary," said Wally.
"Come on, Norville!" They left Bobgoblin
with the mashed potatoes.

Wally and Norville found the swamp.
But Stan of the Swamp wouldn't let
them take any mud.
"Mine!" said Stan.

Stan said he would give Wally and Norville some mud if they gave him something to eat.

"I only eat worms and succotash," said Stan. **Succotash** rhymes with **bash**!

"Succotash!" said Wally. He waved his magic stick, and a plate full of succotash appeared. Stan dug in and let Wally take some mud.

Next, Wally and Norville needed
slime from a lightning snail. They
found the snail—but it was
too fast to catch!
Wally waved his magic stick.
"Dash!" he shouted.

Wally and Norville ran super fast.

They caught up to the lightning snail and got a blob of slime for their beaker.

They passed Bobgoblin, who was now trying to scare Norville with a pink teddy bear.
"Not scary!" said Wally.

The last thing on the list was a flower from the top of the Ice Volcano. Wally and Norville were flying to the top when the volcano began to erupt! "We need something to protect us!" cried Wally.

The only thing he could think of that rhymed with **bash** was **trash.** He waved his stick, and a trash can appeared. The lid made a perfect shield!

Bobgoblin followed Wally and Norville to the top of the mountain.

Wally and Norville reached the flower. But it was frozen! They needed to find a way to melt it.

Just then, Bobgoblin popped out from behind an ice wall with a marshmallow. He thought the marshmallow would scare Norville. It didn't. But Norville hiccupped fire . . . and unfroze the flower!

Wally and Norville added the flower to the
beaker and went back to Ogre Doug's house.
The mixture was finally ready! Wally poured
a drop on Norville's nose.

It worked! Norville's hiccups disappeared!
But just then—*hiccup*. Wally got them! Now
they needed to find a cure for the troll hiccups!